Albany Featherstonehaugh Major

Sagas and Songs of the Norsemen

Albany Featherstonehaugh Major

Sagas and Songs of the Norsemen

ISBN/EAN: 9783742817846

Printed in Europe, USA, Canada, Australia, Japan

Cover: Foto ©Andreas Hilbeck / pixelio.de

More available books at **www.hansebooks.com**

SAGAS AND SONGS

OF THE

NORSEMEN

BY

ALBANY F. MAJOR

LONDON

DAVID NUTT IN THE STRAND

MDCCCXCIV

CONTENTS

SONGS OF THE NORSEMEN

SONGS OF THE ENGLISH

SONGS OF THE NORSEMEN

THE SAGA OF ASMUND EYVINDSSON, ODIN'S MARTYR

TOLD IN ALLITERATIVE VERSE.

UNDER Yggdrassil, the ash-tree famous,
The Gods were gathered together in council,
For a rumour had reached them of rivals uprisen,
Strange Gods and strong, to sweep them away.
Fast by their doom-stead the fountain of Urdar
Sang and sparkled, of streams the purest,
And above it Yggdrassil, oldest of trees,
Wailed in the wind with a warning voice.

Out spake the Sisters whose silent fingers
Weave ever the weird of the world in their loom :
Far had they fathomed the fates unborn
And read the runes and the riddle of Time :
"Hearken, ye High Ones ! Hard is our tale ;
Fain would we fashion you fairer tidings !
Alas for the lips no lie can sully,
When a Norn's foreknowledge brings nought but pain !

Your race is run ; your rule o'er the Norland,
Doomed to destruction, must dwine and dwindle,
Waning away, as the worship of Christ
On its ruins uprises to rule the world."

The doom was delivered, but dauntless they faced it,
And Odin made answer amidst of the doom-ring :
"There are true men and tried put their trust in the
    Æsir
And in bicker of battle the bright sword shall gleam.
Stubborn and stark shall the strife be, whose prize is
The crown of our kingdom. If Christ would o'er-
    throw us,
His gospel of goodwill must garner in slaughter
And its followers enforce it with fire and with sword."

        *   *   *   *   *

In helm and hauberk and harness of battle
King Olaf upheld it, an armed apostle ;
War-gear he wore, as he went on his mission,
Mail shirt for monk's robe, a menacing helmet
For the shaveling's shorn crown, while his sharp gleam-
    ing brand
Was the cross he upheld, as he cruised round the skerries.

So by fjeld and by fjord was the new faith sown
    broadcast,
Preached by the priests as a promise of mercy ;

While the King bade men curtly : "Come ! choose as
    I bid,
Battle or baptism, bible or sword !"

Though his word was unwelcome, 'twas worse to
    oppose him,
Or the faith forced upon them refuse at the sword's
    point.
So men bowed at his bidding, bent their pride,
Kissed the cross and cast off Odin.

There was a Sea-king, sage and stalwart,
Blithest at banquet, boldest in fray,
Asmund, Eyvind's son, Earl of the Nine Isles,
Whose hall rose high on the holm of Thorey.
Craving his counsel came men to seek him,
Bore him the story and begged of him rede,
Whether to yield to the yoke of King Olaf,
Or buckle on byrnie and brave his wrath.

Up rose Asmund in ire from his high seat,
Burst into bitter speech, burning with anger ;
Free-born and fearless, his fiery temper
Despised submission and spurned to yield.

"If Olaf o'erthrow me, upholding in battle
The faith of my fathers, aforetime unquestioned,

Me vanquished the Valkyrs to Valhall will carry,
Where undying in Asgard the Æsir hold sway.
What of this White Christ? When have we known him?
He has not helped us, or heeded us praying!
The gods of our grandsires all good things have given,
The Æsir in Asgard and the white-armed Asynjor.
Odin Allfather, who on Air-throne high seated
Broad lands beholdeth below him out-spread;
He giveth all good things; he gildeth our lives
With fame in the fight and the fulness of praise.
Swift is his sight; never swerveth his justice,
Dealing to divers men as their desert is;
Gold-bright glory he gives to the hero,
To the Skald song-meed, shame to the coward.
Ving-Thor the thunder-god, Thrudheim's master,
Lord of the hammer and hurtling chariot,
Foe to the Frost-giants, friend to all brave men,
The strong god whose stroke shall destroy the world-
    snake.
Tyr who tamed Fenris, the terrible wild wolf,
Nor flinched from his fangs when they fettered him
    down;
Goodly the guerdon he giveth in battle,
Crowning with victory valour and might.
Ægir the ancient, that under the billow
Holds sway o'er the swan's bath, our swift keels up-
    bearing,

That furrow the fallow fields of brine,
Sailing the salt sea in storm or calm.
Baldur the beautiful, brightest of Æsir,
Yet doomed to the dark, drear dwelling of Hel ;
For with hapless hand shall Hödur slay him,
Lured by a lie and Loki's craft.
These are the gods that my grandsires worshipped ;
These are the gods that have guerdoned my days ;
These gods are my gods ! Choose ye god and leader !
Odin and Asmund, or Olaf and Christ ! "

His voice rang in roof-tree and rafter, a clarion
To call up high courage and cast out despair,
As he stood by his high seat, a Sea-king to follow,
To fight for, to fall with, to feast with in Valhall.

Spell-bound they sat on the settles beneath him,
Those wolves of the war play, wave-riders, sword-
  wielders,
Cunning in counsel, and crafty in ambush,
But daring in danger and desperate in fight ;
Huge limbed, heavy handed, they hearkened like
  children,
Till he ceased and with swift eyes sought out every face ;
Then, unsheathing their sharp blades, they shouted in
  answer :
" Odin and Asmund ! Aoi ! for the onset ! "

So Asmund the Earl an arrow took,
Split it and sought out the swiftest of runners,
Torfig the tireless, his token to carry,
Speed through the country and spread the tidings.

By fjord and by fjeld, by forest and moorland,
Outracing the reindeer, ran Torfig unstaying,
Holding on high, as he hurried along,
That message for men to muster in arms.
Through the pinewoods he passed, where the winds
        pipe unceasing
And moan like the mournful music of ocean ;
He ferried the fjords, that far inland
Lap the lone feet of the lofty hills ;
Mountain and moorland and meadow he traversed
To fortress and farmstead and farthest saeter,
And wide went the word that war was afoot,
Till each house and homestead had heard the summons.

Was many a man the message heard,
Who found fresh heart, flung fear aside,
Braced on byrnie, buckled sword on,
Took spear and shield and sought the Earl.

News came to the King, as in Kormdal he lay,
That Asmund had armed to oppose his decree ;

So he mustered his men and manning a fleet
Sailed o'er the sea to seek the foe.

Now face to face the fleets are met,
The shield-hung ships with shining prows,
With men of mettle and might on board
And led by leaders of lineage high.
Lashed in a line the longships bounded
Over the eddying ocean billows,
Closed with a crash of creaking ribs
'Mid the wail of the wind o'er the wan gray surge.

End on end those ocean horses
Grided and ground and grappled together;
Blithe up the bulwarks the boarders clambered
And fierce grew the fight on the forecastles tall.

Brightly burned the flame of battle;
Falchions flashed; the feathered arrows
Ceaseless showered like snow in winter;
Hissed on high the hurtling spears;
Shields were shattered; mail shirts cloven;
Brands bit hard on burnished helmets;
Fierce the fray; but foremost Asmund
Boldly bore the brunt of fight.

But vain was his valour ; the vantage still
Clung to the cause that the King maintained ;
For Olaf's fleet out-numbered the Earl's
And Fortune frowned on the faith of Odin.

So ship after ship in the shock of fight
Was cleared of her crew and cut adrift,
And, loosed from their lashings, the longships floated
Far from the fight on the flow of the tide.

But, like wolves that worry a wounded bear,
The keels of the King closed in on the Earl's ;
Thick and thicker they thronged about her,
The grim death-grapple kept growing fiercer.

Thrice were they thrust back, but thrice they rallied,
Gathered fresh forces and flung them aboard her,
Swarmed o'er the bulwarks and swept before them
The few that were left to fight for Odin.
Fiercely they fought, but fell outnumbered,
Till Asmund alone upheld the battle,
As he stood on the steaming, blood-stained deck
At bay with his back to the broken mast.

His shield was in shards, his shirt of mail
Cloven and pierced and clotted with gore,

Hewn from his helm was the hawk of gold
That he bore as a blazon when boune for fight.
But his heart beat high, his hand smote sure,
The blade of his battle-axe bit full keen ;
The foe, as he fought, fell back dismayed
And shrank from the shock of his shining steel.
But they ringed him around with a rampart of shields
And, walling him in like a wolf in the toils,
Beat down his blade and, bearing him under,
Fettered him fast by the feet and hands.

So the conquering King at the close of day
Leaping aland, the lord of fight,
In the house of the foeman his harness doffed
And rested his limbs from the labours of war.

In the hall on the holm high feast was set,
The red wine ran, the revel grew,
As the King and his warriors wassailed together,
Carousing to Christ and the conquering cross.
In brimful beakers the burly warriors
Pledged the priests who had prayed for their cause,
And in mighty measures of mead and ale,
To Odin's downfall they drank together.

Arrayed in robe and rochet and pall
Sat Bishop Basil beside the King,

A crafty confessor in counsel skilled,
Wary and wise and winning of speech.
As freely the wine flowed round the board
In Olaf's ear he uttered a word ;
Then the royal ring-giver rose in his place
And bade the Earl be brought before him.

When stark and stalwart he stood in their midst,
Friendless, but fearlessly facing the throng,
"Give ear," cried King Olaf, "to all I say,
And counsel me cunningly, comrades mine !
From the sword and the slaughter we spared this
    Earl,
Fain of his friendship ; and free shall he be,
If he bow him to Christ and the cross we bear,
Forsaking frankly his false god Odin ! "

Out burst at once an answering shout,
With that King Olaf to Asmund cried :
" Behold in our bounty the boon we offer,
Proffer of pardon and peace at our hands ! "

But Asmund the Earl made answer swift :
" The gifts of the gods have I garnered oft ;
If I abandon Odin and Thor,
What crowning gift has Christ to offer ? "

Then Bishop Basil began his say ;
How Christ came down and was crucified,
How He rose to reign in His realm above
And with Him in weal are His worshippers all.
" In goodly garments on golden thrones
They sit and sing, those Saints who died
Baptised and bearing on brow the sign
Of the cross that shall conquer the kingdoms of earth.
The false creeds of old have we flung to the winds ;
Odin and all his accursed crew
Are demons dire that destroy the souls
Of folk who refuse the faith we preach :
For dying they dwell in a drear abode
Of famine and flame, where those fiends hold sway,
Torn with torments and tortured for ever
In Hell's grim halls, where hope is dead."

Pondered Earl Asmund and presently answered :
" First of my fathers ! unfold me their doom !
Those high-souled heroes, who held by the faith
Of Allfather Odin in olden time.
They lived their lives in the light of the sun,
Gilded with glory and gallant renown ;
Laughed and laboured for love of the gods
And the folk that they fostered with favouring care.
Then, in fulness of time at the Fates' decree,
Lightly they laid down the load they had borne,

And with helm on head and harness on back
Fell in fight on the field of Odin."

Bitter and brief was the Bishop's speech :
"Pagan they perished !   Now, parched with flame,
They dwell with the damned, where devils in Hell
Rend and rive them and rack them with torments."

Loudly and long laughed out the Earl :
"Better, O Bishop, to burn with them,
Than dwell and drink in the doomstead of Christ,
Who has forced down my fathers to flaming Hell.
But I trow that the tale thou tellest is false,
For in Asgard Allfather Odin reigns ;
He worthily welcomed my warrior sires
And, I ween, I shall wend by the ways they trod.
In vaulted Valhalla those valiant kings
Sit on tall settles beside the gods,
Feasting and filling with foaming mead
The beakers that brighten the board of Odin.
Ever have I at Allfather's hands
Won goodly guerdon ; I give him my life.
Baptise ye the babes, not bearded men !
I fling back thy favours, nor fear thee, King Olaf !"

Up rose Olaf and answered in wrath :
"Baptised shalt thou be in the briny wave,

And thy carcase cast to the kites of the air,
Dishonoured in death, like the dog thou art."

So the King commanded ; his carles obeyed.
'Twixt strand and sea a stake they drave,
Where the ebb uncovered an islet of rock
That at flood lay far 'neath the foaming tide.
There bound in his bonds they brought the Earl,
Lashed him and left him to linger and die,
While the cold sea came creeping and crawling to
       land,
Mournfully moaning among the rocks.

Then in haste to the hall they hied them back,
Wine and wassail went round again ;
Goblets glittered and gushed the mead,
As they drank to his death and the downfall of
       Odin.

Without the south-west wind was moaning,
Sweeping up stormily, salt with its race
O'er the billowy breast of the briny sea,
As landward it lashed the leaping waves.
It cut off the curling crests of the billows,
Sending the scud like smoke down the blast,
And the dappled sea-horses were driven before it
And rushed with a roar up the rugged strand.

But over the uproar of ocean that thundered
And the wail of the wild wind, waking the echoes,
Like a clarion of silver a clear voice rose
And rang in the raftered roof of the hall.
It startled the King, as he sat on his high seat,
It startled the Bishop beside him seated,
It startled the swordsmen on settle and bench,
That voice that vied with the voice of the storm.
Loud when the wind lulled the listeners heard it,
They heard it at height of the wild hurly-burly,
Rising and ringing and rolling in
From the isle where Asmund awaited his doom.
Biding a bitter fate, bound in the darkness,
The champion of Odin was chanting his death-song ;
The winds bore it wide and the waves were his
      harpers,
Swelling the swan-song he sang to the night.

" Death ! I defy thee and dauntless confront thee,
Who ofttimes unflinching have faced thee in battle ;
Now dost thou near me when night and storm lower
And the winds and waters are warring around.
My curse on the White Christ, the cruel and ruth-
      less ;
On the King who has cast me forth conquered to die ;
On the faith that with falchion and firebrand he
      preaches,

Forcing on free necks the foul yoke of thralls!
Nay! curses they need not! They never shall
    triumph;
The arms of King Olaf shall not avail him:
Not long shall Christ crown him, but, crushed by his
    foemen,
He shall drain out the death-draught I drink here
    before him.
All my life have I laboured for love of my
    people;
The gold that I garnered I gave again freely:
In battle I blenched not; broke never a promise;
Feared never a foeman; forsook not a friend.
To Odin Allfather I ever gave worship;
Soon shall I see him high-seated in Asgard:
The High One will hail me, his hand-maidens crown
    me
With golden-bright glory, the gift of his hand."

Shriller and shriller was shrieking the tempest;
The roar of the ocean rose hoarser and hoarser;
Out leaped a lightning flash, lividly gleaming,
And burst with a blaze on the blackness of night;
Then with clang and clatter the clap of the thunder
Rang and re-echoed and rolled through the heavens;
But, when the din had died in the distance,
The song on the skerry had ceased for ever.

Hushed was the high-roofed hall with awe,
Till the King cried out with a cruel smile :
"Satan has seized his soul to-night,
And the carrion we'll cast to the kites to-morrow."

Without the wail of the wild wind ceased ;
The angry ocean assuaged his wrath ;
Hushed lay the house in heavy sleep
And the weary night wore slowly away.

Grayly were gleaming the gates of the morning,
Flushed with the first faint rose of dawn,
With wan light waking the world, as it lay
Drowsy and drowned in the darkness of night.
The gray light gleamed and glanced on the ebbing tide,
Shone and shimmered, where shallow pools lay
In the rifts of the rock and the wrinkles that furrowed
The bare stretch between of the brown sea-sand.

Eastward the mountains arose in silence,
Black 'gainst the brightness that broadened behind them,
Their high peaks piercing the pale blue sky,
Their roots fringed with fretwork of fire and gloom :
For the day-dawn came flooding the dusky recesses
Of the sombre fir-forests on flank and shoulder,
Till boles and branches were broidered in splendour,
As the radiant sun rose to rejoice the world.

Under the early light over the sea-strand
The carles of the King came forth from the hall,
To fling the dead forth to the fowls of the air ;
The doom of a dog, decreed the Earl !
Gaunt in the gray light the grim stake was standing,
But the ropes that hung round it were riven apart,
For the flash of the lightning had fallen upon it
And Asmund the Earl had escaped their hands.

Never in Norway at high noon or mirk night,
Sunrise or sunset, did men see him living ;
The waves of the wan sea ne'er washed up his body,
For Olaf to wreak the revenge he had sworn.
The High Gods had heard him and, hastening from
    Asgard,
Rode on the storm-rush to rescue their champion ;
And, bursting his bonds ere the boiling sea whelmed
    him,
Odin Allfather took Asmund home.

THE FIRST CHRISTMAS IN NORWAY

A YULETIDE LEGEND.

AMBROSE, a priest of God, went forth from Rome
  To preach Christ's gospel to a heathen land.
With sandalled feet the snowy Alps he clomb,
  Traversed the German forests, staff in hand,
  And sailed for Scotland from the Frisian strand :
But tempests drave the vessel far astray,
And wrecked her on the coast of Norroway.

Ambrose, alone of all the shipmen, won
  The land alive and, spent with suffering, gained
The generous roof of Biorn Sigurd's son,
  A mighty sea-king, who in Aardal reigned
  O'er fjord and fjeld.   Thereafter he remained
Guest of that bounteous board the summer through,
Since at his hand was work for him to do.

For heathen was the land and, blind of sight,
  Its people prayed to Odin and to Thor,
Fierce gods who joyed but in the storm of fight,
  And hated peace and loved the arts of war.
  But Ambrose taught them of his precious lore,

Till by his wise discourse and blameless life
He won the ear of Herfrid, Biorn's wife.

Thence her wild husband, unto whom she clung
    Like graceful ivy to a rugged oak,
Heard the sweet words that fell from Ambrose' tongue,
    And, for his wife's sake, listened with his folk,
    Until he felt the truth that in him spoke.
So, ere the autumn, Biorn was baptised
And, with his followers, worshipped the White Christ.

The days wore on till Yuletide drew anigh,
    That had a time of mirth and feasting been
O'er all the North. "But those days are gone by."
    Said Ambrose : "Christian men their thoughts must
        wean
    From all such toys, and wear a sober mien
Mid earth's vain pleasures, and their souls prepare
To celebrate Christ's birth by fast and prayer."

Biorn and Herfrid gave unwilling heed,
    Deeming it truth because he told them so :
Yet, in their heart of hearts, they were agreed
    Such trappings seemlier were for times of woe ;
    And fitter far that song and tale should flow,
And sounds of joy be heard from hill and plain,
Since angels sang when Christ came down to reign.

Now on Yule-eve it fell that Ambrose went
  To a lone chantry in a wooded glen,
Built for his use, where many an hour he spent
  In prayer and penance, far from mortal ken,
  Wrestling with Satan for the souls of men :
Yet was he pledged to come ere night and share
The vigil they must keep of fast and prayer.

White was the earth with the deep winter snows
  And the keen frost bit like a warrior's sword ;
And while he tarried, a fierce wind arose
  That swept across the mountain tops and roared
  Through the dark pinewoods and adown the fjord,
Drifting the snow before it, fold on fold,
While the wolves howled upon the far-off wold.

Then Biorn, listening to the mingling sounds,
  Cried : " Heaven grant the good priest be bestowed
In some safe shelter !   Hark how Odin's hounds
  Howl on the fells, as though their master rode !
  Surely so wild a storm some ill doth bode ! "
While yet he spake, above the loud uproar
They heard a knocking at the outer door.

They flung it open and, without, there stood
  A one-eyed stranger, blithe of face and bold,
Clad in a kirtle gray and cloud-blue hood,
  Looped round his knotty throat with links of gold
  Wrought in the fashion of the days of old ;

While, 'mid the wind and snow, on wings widespread
Two night-black ravens circled round his head.

" Odin's fair peace be on this house ! " he cried :
    " Biorn ! I crave a boon of thee ; to stay
This night beneath thy roof-tree.   Far and wide
    Have I been travelling since the break of day
    And, if I go, must tread a weary way
Through this wild tempest.   Of thy courtesy
Grant me to share thy Yuletide feast with thee ! "

Biorn made answer : " Welcome, in Christ's name !
    I would not drive away into this blast
My bitterest enemy.   Yet, think no shame
    That we can feast you with no rich repast,
    Although our best is yours !   But we keep fast ;
For we are followers of the White Christ now,
Signed with His holy cross upon the brow."

Lightly the stranger answered with a laugh :
    " And have ye fallen away from Odin's rule
To follow one who thinks it sin to quaff
    A horn of mead and cast off care and dule,
    When men make merry with good cheer at
        Yule ?
So be it !   Yet ye will not think it wrong,
If I beguile the night with harp and song ! "

Blithe was the answer ; for the hours dragged slow,
    While Ambrose lingered.   So the stranger shook
The snow-flakes from his mantle by the glow
    Of the bright fire-light.   Then a harp he took
    And on the settle in the ingle-nook
Sat down, and from the chords drew forth a long,
Mysterious prelude, ere he raised his song.

Weird was the strain, that fitfully at first
    Wailed through the hall, as though a low breeze
        crept
Through whispering pines in summer : then outburst
    A peal of triumph, as his firm hand swept
    Along the harp strings, while his full voice leapt
Swift through the silence ; and the rafters rang
And on his words hung all men while he sang.

He told them firstly of the birth of time ;
    Then, how the Æsir with the Giants warred
And drave them back to realms of snow and rime,
    And fashioned the fair earth ; and man, its lord,
    They gifted with their twin gifts, plough and sword ;
And how to Odin's hall his shield-maids bore
The spirits of the brave, who died in war.

Then turned his song to kings who reigned of old,
    The wise in counsel and the bold in fight :

Strong with bright steel and rich with ruddy gold,
  They walked life's pathway and their days were
        bright
With deeds of glory, while they saw the light :
And, as he sang, each tale of ancient days
Rang back to Odin's and the Æsir's praise.

Spell-bound they sat and listened to the stream
  Of song, until he ceased and cried amain :
"And have those days gone by ? or do you deem
  That, careless of mankind, the Æsir reign
  At ease in Asgard ?   Odin is full fain
Of mighty kings and warriors and his door
Stands in Valhalla open evermore."

Then, springing up, he strode and smote the
        board ;
  And straightway were the empty tables spread
With drinking-horns and beakers, that the hoard
  Of Biorn could not match ; with store of bread
  And flesh of beeves and swine ; a huge boar's head
Grinned with gilt tusks, and bowls of ale and mead
Stood ranged, abundant for a nation's need.

Round turning to the king he cried : "At least
  Grant me this boon, King Biorn ! share with me,
Thou and thy folk to-night, my Yuletide feast !

Think'st thou thy Christ would do as much for
   thee,
  As Odin would for his ? Howe'er that be,
For love of old days fill your beakers up
With mead and to Allfather drain one cup ! "

Thereto said Biorn : " Yea, I know thee now,
   Allfather ! But a wordfast man am I,
And pledged to serve the White Christ by my vow
   Of baptism : and He, Who bore to die
   To save men, of a surety will reply
To thy reproach. Yet, if He make no sign
Before the break of day, I count me thine."

E'en as he spake, a knocking loud and long
   Rang on the door and Ambrose entering cried :
" Is this a Christian house, where heathen song
   Profanes the vigil of the holy tide,
   And Christian sits with pagan, side by side ?
Biorn, I charge thee, drive that man away
And on thy knees for God's forgiveness pray ! "

Swift was the King to answer : " Never, priest !
   Shall Biorn from his roof drive forth a guest ;
And little guilt I deem it here to feast
   After my father's wont. Old ways are best,
   And I am tossed in doubt. Be thy behest

The sign I seek for.   Shall I drain this horn
To Odin, or to Christ, the King new-born?"

But Ambrose beat his breast and tore his hair,
   Crying: "Blasphemer, silence!   From God's light
Wouldst thou turn back to heathendom, or dare
   Profane Christ's birth-tide with an impious rite?
Avaunt, apostate!   May God's curse alight—— "
He paused abruptly; nerveless to his side
His threatening hands fell and his accents died.

For in the air a burst of music rang;
   Clear, as on autumn nights when southward fly
The wild swans; but it seemed that voices sang
   To harping sweet: "Glory to God on high!"
   Then, as they listened breathless, through the
     sky,
Drowning that strain, the storm-blast shrieked anew
And the doors rattled in the gust that blew.

The bolts and bars burst open and a flaw
   Of frost-cold wind went whistling round the hall;
The torches flickered and a thrill of awe
   Fell upon priest and king, on free and thrall;
   The weapons ranged against the shield-hung wall
Clanged in the blast, and through the open door
The wreathing snow drove in across the floor.

Then all was still and for a space the storm
  Folded its furious wings and ceased to blow,
While through that stillness came an angel form
    In robes, whose dazzling whiteness made the snow
    Look black and, entering in into the glow
Of torch and firelight, stood beneath the roof
And gazed on priest and king with mild reproof.

About the cross he bore a glory shone,
  That filled the hall with radiance divine :
And fear fell on them, as they looked upon
    The shining seraph and the sacred sign
    He carried ; and before his glance benign
Fell Ambrose' eyes and Biorn's angry frown
Was smoothed away and all men knelt them down.

But Odin with a scornful countenance
  Rose and looked round upon the kneeling throng ;
Then on the angel flung a haughty glance,
    Saying : "I know thee ; and thy Lord is strong
    And, where he cometh, I must go ere long.
Yet, were these *men* to back me, I would try
Who shall be God in Norroway, Christ or I."

Gently the angel answered : "Go in peace,
  Wild wanderer of the night!" The fierce storm-
    blast

Shrieked, as he reached the door, in glad release ;
    About his airy path the snow drave fast
        And the wolves howled beneath him, as he
            passed.
Far o'er the fells the tempest whirled and wailed
And died away and a great peace prevailed.

Hushed was the hall ; low bowed the adoring priest,
    As the great Seraph cried : " Where heathen mirth
Rang through the land of old, shall Christians feast
    At the glad tide that saw the Saviour's birth ;
    Who came to dwell in sorrow on this earth
That His own joy might rest for evermore
On all those loved ones that His name adore."

Then on the boar's head first his hand he laid
    And signed the cross of Christ above the great
Abundance of that Yuletide feast and said :
    " Let none call impious what I consecrate
    At God's command !   Rejoice and celebrate
A Christmas feast of love with song and praise
To the Almighty Giver of good days ! "

He spake, and with a smile stretched forth his hands
    And blessed them, ere he vanished from their sight.
Straightway the heavens were filled with angel-
        bands,

That with their song and music made the night
Jubilant ; while the moon and stars gleamed bright
In the clear sky over the shining fells
And the dim shadows of the forest dells.

"Good father!" said the King : "Praise thou the
    Lord
    And pray him for us!"   Ambrose joyfully
Offered up worship meet ; then at the board
    Said : "The night wastes and faint with fast are ye ;
    Share we the Christmas meal ! for well we see
All gifts of God are hallowed."   As he spoke
Over the fells the dawn of Christmas broke.

THE BURIAL OF THE SEA-KING

THROUGHOUT the day a stubborn fight had raged
   Upon the bosom of the stormy fjord,
In that fierce war King Harald Fairhair waged,
      Enforcing with the sword

His yoke of thraldom on all Norroway.
   Vainly the banded sea-kings faced his might ;
At length, o'er-mastered in the hard-fought fray,
      They turned to sullen flight.

A wild wind lashed the waters into foam,
   As forth they drave before the freshening breeze,
Till they and Freedom found an island home
      Mid the chill Arctic seas.

*   *   *   *   *

Amid the outmost skerries, where the eye
   Of the broad sea looks in upon the land,
Last of the beaten fleet, two longships lie
      Still tossing by the strand.

There on the blood-stained deck, where, axe in hand,
　He battled till the day was lost and won,
Lies stretched the stoutest champion of the land,
　　King Hunthiof Halfdan's son.

He was the foremost in the weapon play,
　The latest who upheld the failing fight,
And, stricken to the death at close of day,
　　He, last of all, took flight.

Wild is the night ; the sky is overcast,
　Save where the moon shines dim 'mid fleecy clouds ;
And his great dragon, in the rising blast
　　That whistles through her shrouds,

Strains at her moorings : while her crew in haste
　Flit through the darkness, ranging in a ring
Their dead upon the brushwood in the waist
　　Before the dying king.

Then, springing to the shore, they fire the heap
　And loose her from her moorings.　In his hand
King Hunthiof takes the helm, and with a leap
　　The longship clears the land.

A moment can they see her in the storm,
　Fast driving westward through the darkness dread ;
Thick clouds of smoke roll up aloft and form
　　A canopy o'erhead.

Then night enshrouds her in a pall of gloom,
   Till to the watchers, straining through the dark
Their eager eyes to know the hero's doom,
      Outshines a sudden spark ;

And, with a roar and whirl of fiery flakes,
   The flames leap up and show her to their sight
And, wreathing round the pyre like lurid snakes,
      Scatter the shades of night.

Each rope stands out against the flood of flame
   And in the light gleams all the warrior's mail.
What though the prize he wins in Odin's game
      Be death ?   He does not quail,

But steers his longship on that fated path,
   As dauntless as when first he took the helm
And, standing out across the gannets' bath,
      Subdued the viking's realm.

Lo ! bright Shield-maidens float before his sight,
   Eager to take him with his latest breath,
Who lived a king and never blenched in fight,
      And dies a warrior's death ;

Eager to bear him hence to Odin's halls,
   Who, from his throne in Asgard far and wide,
Surveys the shock of battling hosts and calls
      His champions to his side.

So on an unknown course, to realms afar
  Beyond the night, the flaming vessel pressed,
Until the light grew faint and, like a star,
        Sank in the distant west.

Thus sailed the Sea-king, wrapped in smoke and fire,
  On his last voyage across the stormy wave,
The blazing longship for his funeral pyre,
        The ocean for his grave.

GUDRUN

WHEN the glorious North-winds blow
And the earth lies white with snow,
By the fjords I love to go
        Looking west :
Far across the seas I gaze,
O'er the reddening, watery ways,
As the sun through heavens ablaze
        Sinks to rest.

Shoreward through the breakers white
As I stand upon the height,
Olaf, lord of many a fight,
        Dashes fleet :
Burnished mail about him rings
And a battle stave he sings :
Like a falcon swift he springs
        To my feet :

Chanting how he crossed the wave,
How the foemen backward gave,
When he met them with the glaive
      Flashing free :
And my love shines unrestrained,
For those dangers he disdained
And the glory he has gained
      Were for me.

OLAF

WHEN afar I long have warred,
Tired of cruising and the sword,
To my own Norwegian fjord
      North I sail.
Bellying sail and straining oar
Speed us fast ; the breakers roar,
Lashed against the rock-bound shore
      By the gale.

Wondrous fires, as on we row,
Redden all the peaks of snow ;
Pale amid their magic glow
      Shines the moon :
While a maiden robed in white
Stands beneath the Northern light,
Gazing seaward from the height.
      'Tis Gudrun !

Quickly up the cliff I climb
And to her I sing my rhyme,
How for her in fight sublime
   Flashed the sword ;
And the glow of love and light
In her eyes shines true and bright ;
For all toils of flood and fight
   Rich reward !

KING OLAF'S GRAVE

DEEP down in an ocean cave
Lies the Sea-king in his grave,
And there 'neath the restless wave
   He rests for evermore :
He hears not the foeman's cry
O'er the waters shrilling high,
He hears not the breezes sigh,
   He hears not the ocean roar.

When with o'erwhelming might
The heathen burst on his sight,
He knew that lost was the fight,
   But he still refused to fly ;
Long with the Swede and the Dane
He fought on the billowy main,
Till his warriors all were slain
   And nought could he do but die.

Though his " Serpent " floated a wreck,
Yet he bowed not his haughty neck,
But leaped from the blood-stained deck
    Where late he proudly trod ;
As through the wave he sank,
As the salt flood he drank,
One prayer through the waters dank
    He dying breathed to God.

On the seaweed soft he lies,
Never again to rise
Till, ringing loud through the skies,
    Shall sound the blast of doom ;
While, though no lofty nave
Spreads o'er the sculptured grave
That holds the warrior brave,
    Grand is his ocean tomb.

There the mermaids in his hair
Twine the seaweeds rich and rare
And guard his body fair,
    Whence the valiant soul has fled,
As, stretched on the golden sand,
Still mailed, while his good right hand
Tight clenches his trusty brand,
    He sleeps the sleep of the dead.

The sea with her waters warm
Fondles the Sea-king's form,
Safe from each angry storm,
  Safe from the beating surge ;
Whilst, though no death-beds toll
To speed his gallant soul,
The grand unceasing roll
  Of the ocean sings his dirge.

THE SAILING OF THE VIKINGS

On the wild coast
 Of Norroway
High is tossed
 The sparkling spray
By the waters that break
 At the foot of the height,
That frowns on the ocean
 Defying his might.
Where the blue waves
 Of the rifted fjord
Cleave the dark earth
 Like a glittering sword,
A longship is speeding
 And in her there sail
A hundred bold vikings,
 Flashing in mail.

Norroway they leave ;
 Past the cliffs high and sheer
On viking-cruise
 They southward steer ;

Seaward they glide
  On the swell of the tide,
Through the mouth of the fjord
  O'er the breakers they ride.

Black the ship, while along her
  With many a fold
Curls a huge dragon,
  Green, crimson and gold ;
Aloft at the prow
  He rears his fierce head
With fiery eyes
  And jaws lolling red,
While high at the stern
  The dragon's forked tail
Shelters the warrior
  Who steers with its mail.

There hang at the gunwale
  Bright shields in a row ;
Like glittering scales
  In the sunlight they glow :
And the striped sails
  Are filled by the breeze,
And the oars drive the vessel
  Fast over the seas.

Twelve oars on a side
  Furrow the deep;
Stoutly plied,
  They foaming sweep
The waters that leap
  With a terrible shock
At the wave-worn base
  Of the craggy rock.

Aloft on the crag
  A Vala stands,
High to the heavens
  She raises her hands ;
High in the air
  Her arms are cast
And her long, fair hair
  Streams out on the blast.
Her voice clearly rings
  To slow, solemn tunes,
As loudly she sings
  Her mystical runes,
Handed down from past ages
  Through the dim mists of old
And preserved by the sages
  On tablets of gold.

She prays to the Æsir,
  In Asgard who reign,

For victory in battle,
  Fair voyage o'er the main ;
To Niord then prays she
  To swell the great sails
And speed the good longship
  With favouring gales ;
Then prays she to Ægir,
  Who rules o'er the sea,
That from rock and from quicksand
  The ship may 'scape free,
From calm that delays her
  Or tempest that harms ;
Thus prays she.   Then seaward
  Outstretching her arms,
She weaves her wild charms
  O'er the sea, as it raves,
And blesses the longship
  That bounds o'er the waves.

Now from the North
  Swift comes the breeze
And whirls the ship forth
  Afar o'er the seas.
The vikings bend forward
  And tug at the oar ;
Behind the cliffs lessen
  And dim grows the shore.

Fainter and fainter
   The Vala's weird song
O'er the swell of the waters
   Is carried along ;
Still fainter it comes
   And at last dies away :
Then nothing is heard
   But the plash of the spray,
The sound of the oars
   As they dip in the wave,
Of the ripples as round
   The stout vessel they lave.

Then the vikings all vow
   By the hammer of Thor
To hold by each other
   In peace or in war ;
To follow their leader,
   Where'er he may go,
And never to falter,
   Or blench from the foe.
One last look at the shore
   Of the far Norroway,
Then southward once more
   They hold on their way :
Swift is their flight,
   As to battle they haste,

On to the fight
  O'er the watery waste,
With the oar in one hand,
  Ever fearless and free,
In the other the brand,
  True kings of the sea.

LEAPING THE BOOM

THE spars and the cordage are creaking,
   The oars sweep the waves with a swirl,
As Olaf, the Skald and the Sea-king,
   Flees away with the child of the Earl.

In the castle are wrath and commotion,
   The warriors flash down to the fjord,
The ships are thrust into the ocean
   And the Earl and his men are on board.

The ships o'er the breakers are dancing,
   As they fling out the sails to the breeze,
The oars through the billows are glancing
   And the spray is tossed up from the seas.

Far ahead on the foam-crested water
   A longship bounds down with the tide ;
On her deck is the Earl's beauteous daughter
   With Olaf the Skald at her side.

She trembles and clings to his shoulder
   And her father's fierce anger she fears,
But the arms of her lover enfold her
   And his voice whispers love in her ears.

Now seaward he anxiously gazes,
   As he leans on the hilt of his sword ;
Then the glittering blade he upraises
   And points to the mouth of the fjord,

Where the waves of the ocean are foaming
   On a boom that is barring their way.
His warriors gaze long through the gloaming,
   Then sternly prepare for the fray ;

For behind them the longships on-speeding
   Scud down with the freshening blast :
The Earl in the "Dragon" is leading
   And gains on the fugitives fast.

But Olaf the Skald never blenches,
   As he cries with a smile on his lip :
"Two oarsmen to each of the benches,
   The rest to the stern of the ship ! "

Her prow rises clear of the billows,
   While her stern in the sea is sunk deep ;

D

The stout ashen oars bend like willows,
　　As she makes at the boom with a leap.

Then upon it she grates through the surges
　　And the whole of her keel is laid bare,
As out of the wave she emerges
　　And a moment hangs poised in mid air.

But forward the ballast is shifted
　　And the seamen bound swift to the fore ;
A moment she quivers up-lifted,
　　Then seaward she slowly heels o'er,

Until, moving swifter and swifter,
　　Down the boom to the ocean she slides ;
The waves leap up foaming and lift her,
　　And into the billows she glides.

Then northward and seaward she dances,
　　On into the gathering gloom,
As the Earl round the headland advances
　　And makes with his ships at the boom.

But his longships all fail to leap over
　　And, long ere they hew it in twain,
The darkness enshrouds the sea-rover,
　　As he skates o'er the limitless main ;

And shrilly the wind whistles o'er him,
   While beneath the waves whiten and curl,
As he sails with the wide world before him,
   And beside him the child of the Earl.

THE RIME OF SIR KARI

SIR KARI rideth through the land,
  Sheathed in steel that shimmers bright ;
Helm on head, his trusty brand
On his thigh and in his hand
  The tough, keen lance that cleaves the fight.
Sir Kari rideth through the land.

Sir Kari cometh to the court,
  Princess Thyra's fame flies wide ;
Fair of face, but proud of port,
Love-lorn wooers are her sport :
  For her sake have many died,
And Sir Kari cometh to the court.

Sir Kari wooeth the fair princess,
  Knightliest he of her suitors all !
The old Queen murmurs in distress :
" Heaven shield him from her wilfulness !
  Pity so goodly a youth should fall ! "
But Sir Kari wooeth the fair princess.

Sir Kari rideth to griesly strife
  'Mid the dank, gray mists of the wind-swept wold ;
For never a wooer may call her wife,
Till the Troll-king lieth bereft of life,
  Where he weaves weird spells 'mid his hoarded gold.
Sir Kari rideth to griesly strife.

Sir Kari lingers. What news i' the air ?
  Full oft the princess seeks the gate.
Wan is her face, that was once so fair,
And her lips are moving in silent prayer,
  Since love has mastered her heart—too late—
For Sir Kari lingers. Ill news i' the air !

Sir Kari rideth back from fight.—
  Smile, O princess, our fear was vain !
But his eyes are glassy, his face is white,
And his charger shivers and cowers with fright,
  For the hand of a dead man grasps his rein !
Sir Kari rideth back from fight.

Sir Kari lieth aneath the mould,
  And the princess sorrows in anguish sore :
She has shorn her locks that were sun-swept gold,
She has taken the veil, and the dismal fold
  Of the "Silent Nuns" hides a dead life more ;
  And Sir Kari lieth aneath the mould.

A SONG OF TWO KINGS

THE king wears a royal crown,
   That is wrought of the red, red gold,
And he sits on his throne in the town
   In the midst of his courtiers bold ;
And he holds out his sceptred hand,
   As he points to his fields with glee :
" I am king of the rich, deep land ;
   Let who will rule the barren sea ! "

The king wears a helm of steel,
   That has glittered in many a fight,
And he sits in his oar-driven keel,
   As she skates o'er the billows white ;
And he cries to his vikings free,
   As the tempest above him raves :
" I am king of the foamy sea
   And the kings of the land are my slaves ! "

The king of the land feasts high
   At the board where the beakers shine,
And the song and the tale flow by,
   As he drinks of the rich red wine ;

But hushed are the feast and the glee,
   When there enters a scout in haste :
"Up, king ! for the wolves of the sea
   Are come o'er the watery waste."

The sea-king stands by the mast ;
   His sword in his hand shines bare
And he shouts to the shouting blast,
   As his flag floats out on the air ;
The raven has flapped his wings,
   For he scenteth afar the fray,
And the wind in the cordage sings
   And the oars drive hard through the spray.

The king of the land rides forth
   With his spears to the strife on the strand ;
The sea-king is out of the North,
   He has beached his ship on the sand :
They have met and the helm of steel
   Has crushed the crown of gold,
And the king of the land is a meal
   For the grim, gray wolves of the wold.

With a clashing of sword on shield
   The king of the sea they greet,
Lord of the foughten field,
   With his foemen dead at his feet ;

And he cries on Odin and Thor,
   As he wipes his blood-stained brand,
And he stands 'twixt sea and shore,
   The king of the sea and the land.

SPRING TIME IN THE VIKING DAYS

NORWAY.

SPRING and the sun are returning and winter is past;
    Aoi !
The bonds he has flung round the earth are loosened
    at last ; Aoi !
  Soft blows the breeze o'er the mountain tops, melt-
    ing the snow ;
  Swoln are the rivers and, foaming and frothing, they
    flow
  Seaward. Right weary are we of the land and it's,
    Oh !
For the creak of the wind in the cordage aloft and the
    flap of the sail by the mast ! Aoi !

Seaward the breezes blow, bidding us idle no more,
    Aoi !
Curling and flecking with foam-flakes the wide ocean
    floor. Aoi !
  Earth was our sojourn awhile, but the sea is our
    home.

Hark ! how he calls us on viking-cruise over the foam,
  As, surging and seething, he grinds at the beach. We
    will roam,
And our longship no longer shall yearn for the waves,
  as she frets high and dry on the shore.   Aoi !

Gather and run her down over the rollers of pine, Aoi !
Down to the foam-tossing breast of the welcoming
    brine.   Aoi !
  Upward to clasp her he flings his white arms in wild
    glee ;
  Downward she plunges, till knee-deep we stand,
    with the sea
  Laughing and leaping and curling round ankle and
    knee.
Oh ! sweeter the smell of the salt sea-waves than the
  scent and the savour of wine !   Aoi !

Bind on the helm and the mail shirt and buckle the
    sword !   Aoi !
All man can need for the fray or the feast is aboard.
    Aoi !
  Leap to the deck and without, in a glittering row,
  Hang up your shields round the gunwale, till change-
    ful they show
  As the scales of a serpent that slides through the sun-
    light aglow,

Or coils his huge folds in the gloom of the woods round
    the gold he has heaped in his hoard !   Aoi !

Cast off the ship from the land and the white sails
    unfurl !   Aoi !
Run the oars out ! then away ! with the waters aswirl,
    Aoi !
  With a rush of the blades through the water, the
    song of the breeze
  In the curve of the sail and the cordage, while,
    blending with these,
  Laugh the ripples awash round the prow, as it
    cleaves through the seas,
And the foam-flakes go dancing back far in our wake
    and before us the waves leap and curl.   Aoi !

There's many a king in the holds of the south shall
    grow pale ; Aoi !
Many a warrior, the prop of a kingdom, shall quail ;
    Aoi !
  When we drive with the wind in our sails and their
    land on our lee,
  And their watchers have sighted our ships and,
    screaming with glee,
  The ravens and kites circle wide, as, kings of the sea,
We come leaping aland on the crest of the wave and
    winged by the breath of the gale.   Aoi !

Boundless the sea lies before us and we are its lords;
    Aoi!

Kings of the world and the wealth that such empire
    affords; Aoi!

  Lords of the sea by the sweep of our sceptre, the oar;

  Kings of the world by the deeds we have wrought,
    deeds of war,

  When the kings of the land and their armies reeled,
    blenching before

The push of our shields and the thrust of our spears
    and the sway and the stroke of our swords. Aoi!

Dim in the distance the land fades, the ocean rolls
    high; Aoi!

Our longship alone wings her way 'twixt the sea and
    the sky; Aoi!

  The surges beneath answer back to the voice of the
    gale,

  Mirthful and mournful by turns, boding blessing or
    bale;

  But we reck not what doom shall befall us, as daunt-
    less we sail,

For the Norns in their hands hold the thread of our
    lives and we sail and Allfather is nigh. Aoi!

THE SEA-KING'S STORM SWOOP

There's an oar in every hand
   And a sword at every side,
As fast towards the land
   Across the waves we glide ;
The storm shrieks at our back
   And whirls us on our way ;
Above the sky frowns black,
   While the sea is ashen gray,

The waves run ridged with white
   And the storm goes shrieking high ;
But the sea is our delight
   And the wind is our ally :
Wolves of the wave, world-wide
   The winds have blown our fame ;
And who but we dare ride
   The tempest none can tame ?

The tough mast bends and creaks
   Beneath the bellying sail ;
The salt spray wets our cheeks,
   Whirled upwards by the gale,

As we scud before the wind
   Towards the foemen's shore,
While the tempest looms behind
   And in front the storm of war.

But we reck not of its wrath
   As we whirl before the blast ;
Our wake shows white with froth,
   The oars go flashing fast ;
On for the land we press,
   Till through a mist of spray,
Rounding the wave-worn ness,
   We sweep into the bay.

In front of us the foe
   Along the coast-line swarm ;
A few short hours ago
   They blessed the gathering storm ;
But I trow their hearts grew pale
   And they cursed us bitterly,
When they spied our swelling sail
   'Twixt the cloud-rack and the sea.

The breakers shorewards curl
   And on their crest we bound,
Till in a wash and swirl
   Of waves we take the ground ;

Our curved keel ploughing deep
    Furrows the gray sea-sand,
And from the deck we leap
    And wade towards the land.

The oars aside we cast,
    Nor stay to moor the ship :
Their javelins whistle past,
    But the trustier sword we grip
And, locking shields before,
    Drive at the foe abreast,
A steel-gray wave of war
    With our sword blades for its crest.

The spray and rain and wind
    Against the foe are driven ;
The sword-blades gride and grind
    And shield and mail are riven ;
The blood flows down in streams
    And runs into the sea,
And the circling raven screams
    For the banquet that shall be.

We ride the surging fight
    As we rode the gusty gale ;
Before our blades that bite
    Those land-abiders quail,

With little heart to brave
   So fell a storm of war ;
So we wild wolves of the wave
   Are the lords of sea and shore.

HELGA'S BRIDAL

A LEGEND OF ICELAND.

YOUNG Helga is long in returning
  At evening from milking the kine,
And her cheeks with a bright blush are burning
  And her eyes with a strange lustre shine :
And she pouts at the good housewife's chiding
  That she loiters so late by the way,
When the Trolls, who by daylight seek hiding,
  Prowl out and go hunting for prey.

For Grimnis, the Troll of the Grimfoss,
  Dwelt hard by the farm in his den,
Where the wind in the birch-trees moaned wildly
  And the cataract leaped down the glen.

Young Helga grows cold to the lover
  To whom she has plighted her troth,
And Ari too soon shall discover
  That to wed a mere herdsman she's leth ;

E

For she dreams of the wealthy old bonder,
    Who meets her at eve while she milks,
And she sighs for the farm over yonder,
    Where he's promised to clothe her in silks.

But Grimnis, the Troll of the Grimfoss,
    Laughed loud as he sat in his den,
While the wind and the fall mourned the folly
    That blindeth the daughters of men.

There was fear at the farmstead one gloaming,
    For never did Helga come back ;
Unmilked the sleek cattle were roaming
    And the milk pails lay flung in the track.
Young Ari the herdsman despairing
    Uproused all the dale to his aid ;
All night the red torches went flaring,
    But they found not a trace of the maid.

But Grimnis, the Troll of the Grimfoss,
    No longer sat lone in his den ;
And the wind in the birch-trees wailed sadly
    And the cataract moaned down the glen.

Next evening, with fruitless search weary,
    As Ari went home o'er the fells,
Through a region deserted and eerie
    With the fear of the Troll and his spells,

Lo! away on a great mountain shoulder
     A huge form, half lost in the mists,
Sat kicking its heels on a boulder
     With something it gnawed in its fists.

For Grimnis, the Troll of the Grimfoss,
     Loved to watch from the rocks round his den,
While the wind swept the birch-trees below him
     And the cataract foamed through the glen.

But Ari was fiercely defiant
     Of danger and reckless with grief;
So he called to the grim, griesly giant
     With some hope of unlooked-for relief;
"Ho! Troll of the Grimfoss, I greet you!
     What is it you hold in your hand?
Give me news, an you can, I entreat you,
     If my Helga be yet in the land!"

For Grimnis, the Troll of the Grimfoss,
     Had mountain and vale in his ken,
While the wind in the birches made music
     And the cataract splashed in the glen.

A ghastly grin rippled and eddied
     O'er the face of the Troll, ere he cried;
"Last evening your Helga I wedded:
     And I'm gnawing the bones of the bride!"

With a howl Ari sprang o'er the heather
    And flew up the rocks at the Troll,
Breathing low, as they grappled together :
    " Oh, Christ ! nerve my hands, shield my soul ! "

For Grimnis, the Troll of the Grimfoss,
    Was strong with a strength as of ten ;
Far below the wind howled in the birches,
    And the cataract shrieked from the glen.

All night on the mountain they wrestled ;
    Ari fought with the strength of despair ;
They wakened the birds as they nestled,
    And startled the fox from his lair :
But the Troll's force grew stronger and stronger,
    While Ari's was ebbing away,
Till he felt he could struggle no longer ;
    When behold ! in the east dawned the day.

Ho, Grimnis ! thou Troll of the Grimfoss,
    Canst thou measure the cunning of men ?
Or the shrill wind that sways the birch-branches,
    Or the water that falls through the glen ?

So tightly the Troll's arms were clasping
    Round Ari, as prostrate he lay,
That he could but just murmur, half gasping :
    " Who rides on a white horse this way ? "

Round eastward the Troll glanced, but, seeing
    The dawn like a king on his throne,
With a death-pang that thrilled his whole being
    Was changed to a pillar of stone.

So Grimnis, the Troll of the Grimfoss,
    No longer spreads fear from his den :
But the wind in the birches makes music,
    And the cataract foams through the glen.

CHAPTERS FROM THE HEIMSKRINGLA OF SNORRI STURLUSON

I. KING SKIOLD'S VENGEANCE

Saga I. Chapter LI.

King Eystein of Westfold hoisted his sails,
Hung the shields up round the bulwark-rails,
And upon viking-cruise sailed away
Up the fjord to the bight where Varna lay.

King Skiold of Varna was Eystein's foe :
So the clash of the sword and the twanging bow
Was the music he weened would welcome his host :
But none stood forward to guard the coast.

The women and children had fled in affright
And they found in the town not a living wight :
So they plundered each house and ravaged the land
And slaughtered the cattle upon the strand.

Now Skiold the King was a warlock skilled ;
With Finland magic his breast was filled :
But, for all his cunning, there came to the king
No warning of Eystein's harrying.

So he was away with his followers all,
Courtman and bonder, freeman and thrall,
Up in the pinewoods chasing a bear
That famished had burst from his winter lair.

But, looking by chance from the hills, he spied
The flashing of arms by the water side ;
So he wound his horn to gather his band
And rushed down raging to guard the strand.

But when he got down to the shore of the bay,
Wary King Eystein was off and away ;
And the gleam of his sails was dimly seen
'Twixt the blue of the sky and the ocean green.

King Skiold unsheathed his shining brand,
In a wizard's circle he paced the strand ;
He looked up the mountain, he looked down the fjord,
And wrote on the sand with the point of his sword.

Then he lifted his voice in mysterious runes,
Like the song of foreboding the salt sea croons,
When the waves are at rest and calm are the skies,
But the fishers are watching for storms to rise.

He blew a deep breath in the folds of his cloak,
Then shook it and cried 'mid his wondering folk,
(While a grim smile over his visage flits) :
" King Eystein of Westfold, methinks we are quits ! "

Eystein, sailing with wind and tide,
Sat steering the " Osprey," while close beside
The " Bison " breasted the salt green seas,
And the sails and cordage sang in the breeze.

Within the Earl Isles as they sailed along,
A gust came sudden and swift and strong ;
It took back the sails, they shivered and flapped
And the mainsail sheet of the " Bison " snapped.

A great sea struck her ; her boom swung wide
O'er the " Osprey's " deck, as she sailed beside ;
It swept King Eystein overboard
And he sank to his death in the tumbling fjord.

They cruised about till his corse they found ;
Then home they bore him and raised his mound
In the field at Vodle that seaward looks,
Where the ocean welcomes the ice-cold brooks.

II. SAUER, THE DOG KING

SAGA IV. CHAPTER XIII.

EYSTEIN, king of the Uplands,
   Made war on the Drontheim land,
And he set his son King Onund
   To hold it under his hand ;
But the people rose upon Onund
   And slew him by Sparbo brook :
So with fire and sword King Eystein
   A savage vengeance took.

When crushed they lay beneath him,
   He summoned them to a Thing
And said : " Ye scorn a King's son !
   So choose ye for your king,
Ye dogs and thralls of Drontheim,
   Either Thorer Faxe, my thrall,
Or Sauer, the wary wolf-hound,
   The watch-dog in my hall ! "

He spake with scornful laughter,
   That smote them like a blow.
Fierce anger burned within them,
   But they dared not let it show :

So at length they chose the wolf-hound,
　　For 'twas whispered among them all :
" We shall rid ourselves the sooner
　　Of the dog than of the thrall ! "

Now this tale is told about Sauer :
　　By the craft of a wizard wight
He was gifted with three men's wisdom
　　And gifted with seven men's might ;
And of three words that he uttered
　　He spake the first one plain,
So that all might understand it,
　　But he barked the other twain.

So Sauer, King Eystein's watch-dog,
　　Was king o'er the Drontheim land ;
And he dwelt at Inderoen,
　　Where they built at his command
A fair and stately feast-hall
　　With pillars of carven wood ;
And the name of Saurshoug clingeth yet
　　To the mound whereon it stood.

There he sat on a lofty high-seat,
　　As kings were wont of old,
And he wore a chain of silver
　　And a collar of beaten gold ;

And men hearkened to his dooming,
  And his courtiers sang his praise,
And high in their hands they bore him
  When foul were the weather and ways.

How long he reigned I wot not ;
  But this tale of his death is told :
One gloomy night of winter
  The wolves came down from the wold
And ravined among the folded kine ;
  But the neatherds fled dismayed,
For the famished beasts were many,
  So they ran to the hall for aid.

Then his courtiers egged on Sauer
  With cunning, flattering words
To fall on the savage mountain thieves
  And guard his flocks and herds :
Right royally his courage showed,
  For down from his mound he ran
And into the fold he leaped straightway
  And a furious fight began.

With none to aid he fought so well
  That seven huge wolves he slew ;
But they thronged about so thick and fast
  That, for all that he could do,

The gaunt, gray robbers pulled him down
  And limb from limb they tore.
So Sauer, the wary wolf-hound,
  In Drontheim reigned no more.

A SHIP BURIAL

THORSTEIN THORDSSON lay on the deck
  He never again should tread,
With a spear in his side and a gash in his neck
  And his life-blood spouting red ;
But the light of victory gleamed in his eyes,
  As he marked how the foemen fled :
And the long delight of his days of fight
  Flashed back through his dying brain,
How he guarded his life in the storm of strife,
  When the javelins flew like rain,
And the thrust of the spear and the stroke of the sword
  Was many a warrior's bane ;
Or in warfare waged with the winds that raged
  And the waves that leaped round his ship,
Seaward he steered with the storm in his beard
  And the sea-spray salt on his lip,
While the safety of ship and of seamen hung
  On the rudder he held in his grip.

The eyes of the Sea-king closed in death :
  But his memory lived and the praise

Of his prowess in war, as his friends told o'er
    The fame that had gilded his days,
The fights he had fought and the deeds he had
      wrought,
    As he traversed the fierce world's ways.
They had stood by his side on the field of fight
    And the deck of his ocean-steed ;
In woe and weal they had found him leal,
    A hater of wrong and greed,
Frank and bold and lavish of gold,
    A helper at every need.
So they deemed 'twas an evil day for his friends,
    But a welcome hour for his foes
And a gladsome day for the Gods above,
    When Odin his champion chose ;
While his name and his fame on the earth would live
    As long as the mountains rose.

They hauled his longship high on the shore,
    Never again to sail
Where the sunlight streamed and the seagull screamed
    O'er the home of the spouting whale,
While she leaped o'er the seas, as they curled in the
      breeze,
    Or staggered before the gale.
The oars were shipped and the boats inboard ;
    Then they lowered the lofty mast

And furled her sail, the cloak of the gale,
    And before her the rollers cast ;
Then they hung up their shields round the bulwark rail
    And hauled on the ropes of bast.
Over the strand up the rise of the land
    She went on her latest cruise
To the long, low ness that stretched away,
    Washed by the spray and the dews,
Betwixt the slope of the mountain side
    And the bath of the wild sea-mews.

They drew her along to the end of the ness,
    Till she lay where the burial-howe
Should stand on high 'twixt sea and sky,
    Seaward turning her prow
In a last long gaze o'er those watery ways
    That she never again should plough.
Then with ridgepole and rafter within the waist
    The chamber of death was built,
And within it the King's high-seat was placed
    With its carved arms painted and gilt.
The earth was heaped round the vessel's sides,
    Till flush with her bulwarks it rose ;
Then they went to bring the corpse of the King
    To the place of his long repose.
Shoulder-high he rode on his shield
    And behind him the rest of the slain,

To fare at his side, till the doors were flung wide
  In Valhalla, while Odin was fain
Of a chieftain that came with a crown of such fame
  At the head of so goodly a train.

They set down his bier by the side of the ship ;
  And Einar the Skald stood forth
And told his praise and the deeds of his days
  And his fame that was wide in the North.
O'er the feet of the King he drew stout shoes,
  New-fashioned of untanned hide,
And their thongs he wound and fastened them
    round,
  Then rose from his knees and cried :
" I bind these hell-shoon on Thorstein's feet
  That must traverse the rugged road
That leads past the gloomy kingdom of Hel
  To Odin's glad abode :
Naught I know of binding on shoon
  If ever these loose from his feet ! "
Then they bore him into the burial-house
  In his war-gear all complete,
And the dead on the ground were ranged around
  And he sat in their midst on his seat.

They built up the chamber with plank and beam ;
  And when these rites were done,

Or ever they closed the mouth of the howe,
    Came Gunnar Thorstein's son :
A great rock from the ground he tore
    And lifted it up amain
And dashed it down on the deck of the ship,
    Till her timbers creaked again :
She quivered and groaned from stem to stern,
    While he shouted aloud : " I wis,
There is nought I know of mooring a ship,
    If wind or weather stir this !"

Then high o'er the vessel the earth was heaped
    And a mighty howe they made,
That men should know that there below
    Was a famous chieftain laid :
And, leaving Thorstein to his rest,
    They launched and hoisted sail,
To carry home the news of his death
    And to brew his heirship ale.

So he sits 'mid his dead with helm on head
    And his sword upon his knee,
Lulled by the whispering of the wind
    And the murmuring voice of the sea,
Till the loom of Fate weaves soon or late
    The weird that the world must dree ;
Till Heimdall blows a blast on his horn
    And wakens the dead from their graves,

F

For the wolf breaks loose and the grim Earth-snake
    Uprears his huge bulk from the waves,
While Surtur rides over from Muspellheim,
    And the Jotuns and Trolls from their caves
Flock forth to fight 'gainst the Lords of light,
    And the need of the Gods is sore ;
But, undismayed, they call to their aid
    The champions chosen of yore,
And spears are cast, while Death reaps fast
    On the harvest-field of war.
There is many a life must be spent in the strife
    And the fight shall be fierce and long,
And bitter the woe that the world must know,
    For the powers of evil are strong ;
But the cause of the Gods is the cause of the world,
    The struggle of right against wrong.
So it's well for the champions that march with the
      Gods
    To the battle on Vigrid's plain,
For the dead will be blest in an endless rest,
    And the victors will share in the gain,
When the world is refashioned and evil is dead
    And the High One comes down to reign.

WEAPON SONGS

PRELUDE

Songs we will sing you,
The songs that aforetime
Our fathers sang, facing
The foeman in battle :
Sang to the sound
Of the spear, as it hurtled,
Of the sword, as the shield-board
Fell shattered before it,
Of the battle-axe breaking
The byrnie asunder :
Sang in medley of men
To the music of battle.

The weapons that warriors
Wield on the fight-field,
The war-gear they wear
In the war-play we sing you ;
A spear and a helm song,
A shield and an axe song,
A sword and a byrnie song,
Songs of the Vikings !

A BYRNIE SONG

The sheep to the housewives
   Their fleeces surrender,
Who weave the wool deftly
   And dye it with splendour ;
And maids with lithe fingers,
   For their lovers' adorning,
Weave kirtles an emperor
   Might wear without scorning.

Our sheep are the mountains
   We rob of their treasure,
To forge from their iron fleece
   No soft robes of pleasure ;
Swart smiths are our handmaids :
   The shirts of their weaving
We wear in the death-storm,
   When sharp swords are cleaving.

No garments are goodlier
   To feast in or fight in,
Than the tough shirts of ring-mail
   That warriors delight in ;

Till our death-fight we'll wear them
And, dead, the bright byrnie
Will serve us for death-shroud,
As to Valhall we journey.

A HELM SONG

MANY a polished, dwarf-wrought gem
Decks the monarch's diadem :
Fashioned of the ruddy gold
Won by kings in days of old,
Ermine-lined, it rests, I trow,
Softly on the royal brow.

No rich furs or jewels rare
Deck the gleaming helm I wear :
Wrought of steel and burnished bright
For a lode-star in the fight,
Fair it shineth in good omen,
Hope of friend and fear of foemen.

Golden from its crest upsprings
A broad pair of falcon wings,
That, wide-spread for forward flight,
Flutter in the van of fight.

Where they wave, there lies the way
To the thickest of the fray.

Broad may be the monarch's realm :
But beneath the warrior's helm
His world-kingdom broader lies,
Bounded only by the skies.
Every king that wears a crown
To the helm must bow him down.

A SHIELD SONG

STOUT linden boards faced
    With a hide of tough leather,
And a steel rim about it
    To bind them together !
Door of Odin !   I vaunt thee,
    My bulwark in battle,
When like hail on a hall-roof
    The arrow-showers rattle !

From my first fight in youth
    O'er the field I rode glorious,
On my broad shield uplifted
    By warriors victorious :

With a clash of their swords,
  While the brown strand was reeking
With the blood of the foemen,
  They greeted the Sea-king.

Once more from my last fight,
  When Death proves the stronger,
I shall ride on the shield
  I can carry no longer,
Borne off shoulder-high
  From the field of my glory :
But the fame of the Sea-king
  Shall live long in story.

A SPEAR SONG

No sceptre holds sway
  Like the spear that we fashion :
Sharp steel are our spear-points,
  The tough shafts are ashen.
Bright-faced are our maidens
  And radiant their glances,
But brighter and keener
  The points of our lances.

Hurled forth by strong hands,
   Like a swift falcon winging
His way through the clear air,
   The long shaft goes singing ;
Through shield and through byrnie
   It whistles and hurtles,
As if mail-shirts of warriors
   Were but maids' woollen kirtles.

Like the stiff blades of wheat
   O'er a field that we sowed in,
So thick stand the spears
   On the red field of Odin :
A path through that spear-wood
   To victory we'll cleave us,
Or, dead, in Valhalla
   Shall Odin receive us.

A SWORD SONG

CROSS-HILTED is my sword,
   Two-edged and keen for fight,
And its glittering blade is scored
   With runes of magic might ;

From hilt to point they run,
  Inwrought with golden wire,
And they flicker in the sun
  Like a flame of yellow fire.

They flicker and they glow,
  As our falchions sway and sweep,
When the shield-burg of the foe
  Is the harvest that we reap :
We reap with edges keen
  Till the blood flows out like water ;
And the Valkyries shall glean
  On that harvest-field of slaughter.

So when my time is sped
  And Death has cut me down,
And the Shield-maids bear me—dead—
  From the field of my renown,
There's a hall with bounteous board
  I shall win a long abode in,
Where the champions of the sword
  Are the chosen guests of Odin.

AN AXE SONG

Broad hewer of helmets, shield-biter !
  I praise thee in peace or in war.
In peace, when thy task is the lighter,—
  To cleave the tall trees to the core,—
Thy mighty strokes echo like thunder
  And those kings of the forest must fall,
With their tough fibres riven asunder,
  For the building of longship or hall.

When there's war in the wind and the goodman
  Must march at the war-arrow's call,
And the axe that he plied as a woodman
  Is snatched down again from the wall,
Thy task is the sterner and grimmer :
  For a forest of spears stands arrayed
And the light seems to waver and shimmer
  On helmet and byrnie and blade.

Lo ! the banquet is spread for the ravens
  And the foe are the trees that we fell !
The slaughter grows grim and the cravens
  Go down to the kingdom of Hel ;

The flame of the battle burns brighter,
We wade in a dark crimson sea :
Hard hewer of helmets, broad biter
Of byrnies, my trust is in thee !

SONGS OF THE ENGLISH

HENGEST'S LANDING

A FRAGMENT TOLD IN ALLITERATIVE VERSE.

HENGEST and Horsa, Lords of the White Horse,
Dashing in dragon-ships through the dank sea-mists,
Came on the curl of the foam-crested billows
To the bright shores of Britain, bride of ocean.
For the Roman, when riot racked his dominion
And hordes of heathen hotly pressed him,
Forsook the far island to battle the foe
That menaced the might of the mistress of earth.
So the legions no longer kept law in the island,
Its defenders departed and left it defenceless.

North dwelt fierce nations, that ne'er from the Roman
Had blenched in battle or bowed the knee,
'Mid moor and mountain maintaining the strife,
When the arms of the alien assailed them hottest :
Rejoicing they rose on the rear of the legions
And, bursting the barrier built by Severus,
Southward swept with storm of slaughter,
Fleshing of falchions and kindling of flames.

Noised was the news from north to south
And men were mustered to meet their raid :
But Vortigern's valour availed them nought
And the lawless hordes laid waste the land.
But the king took counsel and, casting about
For aid and alliance at alien hands,
Drew to him heroes to haste to his side
Over the wild waste of wan water:

There cruised on the south coast three keels of the
     English :
(Men style them Saxons in song and story ;)
Far went the fame of the fights they had won,
Those wolves of the wave whose joy was war.

They sailed the sea, when the storm blew high,
And drank delight, as they dared its wrath;
They joyed in the jar of hosts that joined
'Mid the ruin and wrack of a reeling world :
Sworded they sat and strained at the oar-bench,
Blithe to battle the tossing billow,
Or to close in the clangour and clash of fight
And with death-grasp grim to grapple the foe ;
Ply rope and rudder and ride the ocean,
Or handle the sword-hilts and hew down the foeman.

To their ships he sent and sought their aid,
Help 'gainst the hordes that harried his land,

Fanned their fierce spirit and fondness for strife
With the largess he lavished of lands and gold.

So Hengest and Horsa hoisted their sails
And steered for the strait where the sea-streams meet ;
The flood-tide flowed and the channel was full
That cuts off a cantle of land from Kent.
The shining shields round the shiprails hung,
As they sailed up the strait to a spit of sand
With breeze fair blowing and, beaching their ships,
Landward leaped to the island strand.

*   *   *   *   *

THE GRAVE

A FRAGMENT.

TRANSLATED FROM THE ANGLO-SAXON.

For thee was a house built
Before thou wert born ;
For thee was mould meant
Ere of mother thou camest :
But not yet is it dight,
Nor the depth of it measured ;
No look has yet reckoned
What length it must be for thee.

One day they'll bring thee
Where thou shalt abide ;
Thee first shall they measure,
Then mete the mould after :
Nor is this house of thine
High built with timbers ;
It is un-high and low
When thou liest within it.

The heel-walls are low
And the side-walls not lofty,
And the roof of it built
To thy breast full nigh.
So thou in the damp earth
Shalt dwell full cold,
Dimly and darkly ;
That den rotteth ever.

Doorless that house is
And dark is't within it ;
There fast art thou dungeoned
And Death holds the key.
Loathly is that earth-house
And a grim one to dwell in,
Where thou shalt dwell
And worms shall devour thee.

Thus art thou laid out,
Most loathsome to friends ;
Nor hast thou a friend
That will fare to thee now,
That will look if thou findest
That house to thy liking,
That will undo the door
And descend to seek thee.

For thou soon must grow loathly
And gruesome to look on,
From thy head soon be reft
The hair that adorned it,
All thy fairness of hair
Forthwith be scattered,
And none with fond fingers
Will fondle it ever.

THE BATTLE OF HASTINGS

THE EVE OF THE BATTLE

The autumn moon shines with a clear, cold light
   In the blue heavens : on the earth below
A rich warm glow of colour floods the height
   Of Senlac, where the watch-fires' fitful glow
Flickers on axe and brand and burnished mail,
   That brighten all the hillside.   Swiftly flow
The horns of foaming mead ; and song and tale
   Resound o'er all the camp with merry din,
As stalwart warriors from hill and dale
   To join King Harold's host come hastening in
And range themselves with his undaunted band ;
   To conquer, or a glorious death to win
Upon the hillside, where in arms they stand
To guard the freedom of the English land.

But from the Norman camp beyond the vale
   Sound chant and psalm, where pious soldiers pray
That the great God of Justice will not fail
   The cause that Rome has blest, but crown the day
With spoil and slaughter to their hearts' content.
   Meanwhile the English whom they thirst to slay

Are feasting round their watch-fires on the bent.
    Just is *their* cause : long since their peace was made
With Heaven ; when forth to guard the isle they
        went
    And grasped the axe and bared the glittering blade :
What time King Harold's war-horns sounded shrill
    And every Englishman himself arrayed
Beneath his banners upon Senlac hill,
To guard the island coast with sword and bill.

Now, seated round the brightly blazing fires,
    They sing old war-songs ; of the glorious fight
Of Brunanburh, and Maldon, where their sires
    Won everlasting fame and put to flight
The valiant hosts of the invading Dane.
    So they too hope before another night
To drive the Normans back across the main,
    Or leave them lying on the gory field,
Cumbering the gloomy valley with their slain :
    At worst they can but fall 'neath sword and shield,
Leaving a name renowned for evermore,
    As men who fought and fell and would not yield,
Although their life-blood streamed from every pore
And all the vale of Senlac swam with gore.

At length is either host in slumber drowned
    And not a sound rings through the silent night,

Save where the sentinels are pacing round
   The watch-fires ; in whose slowly dying light
The English sleep and in their dreams o'erwhelm
   The flying foe.   There in his harness bright
Lies Harold in his tent, the burnished helm
   Upon his head, while ready to his hand
Rests the keen battle-axe that guards the realm.
   So like a king amid his warrior band
He sleeps.   But near and nearer comes the day,
   Fateful to Harold and the English land :
Already faintly shines the twilight gray
That heralds in the morning of the fray.

The watch-fires' ruddy blaze grows sickly pale
   Before the first wan glimmers of the morn.
At length ere sunrise over hill and dale
   Rings the shrill clangour of a warning horn,
Startling to life the silent English camp :
   For from the Norman host a sound is borne
Upon the breeze.   There loud the war-steeds champ
   And clashes steel on steel, as foot and horse
Come pouring forwards with a martial tramp
   And sweep adown the slope in stately course.
With close and serried ranks the vale they fill,
   Out-numbering many times the little force
That waits their fiery onslaught, dauntless still
In arms upon the brow of Senlac hill.

THE FIGHT AT SENLAC

On up the side of Senlac Hill the knights of the
    Normans rode,
And the sacred banner was in their midst, and on
    the footmen strode :
And in the van of the Norman host a giant warrior
    came,
In glittering steel from head to heel, and Taillefer
    was his name.
Alone he rode a javelin-cast the Norman host
    before
And, spurring along, he chanted a song that told of
    the days of yore.
He sang of the dauntless paladins that warred round
    Charlemagne
And of the fight at Roncesvalles, the valiant Roland's
    bane ;
And how the traitor Ganelon the host of the Franks
    betrayed
To the false followers of Mahound in the Pyrenean
    glade ;
And how, too late, the wondrous blast of that en-
    chanted horn
Which Roland wound, as the foe closed round, to
    Charlemagne was borne :

Loud at the close of every stave rang out the cry, "Aoi!"
And the Norman knights, as they came behind, were
    stirred with a martial joy.

Above his head as he galloped along his sword in
    the air he threw
And caught it by the jewelled hilt, then tossed it up
    anew,
Till round his head it seemed to play like a flash of
    lightning bright,
As though some juggler of the East were riding to
    the fight
Before the van of the Norman host and not a belted
    knight.
But forward sprang an Englishman to lay the minstrel
    low ;
Once more did Taillefer high in air his glittering
    falchion throw,
And caught it, as it fell, and smote and clave his
    head in twain ;
So dropped he dead and his blood streamed red over
    the battle plain.

Then a gallant Thane ran forward and whirled his
    axe around
And sprang at the minstrel Taillefer to smite him to
    the ground ;

But his breast was left unshielded, as he lifted his
    axe for the fight,
And Taillefer couched his lance and, as the chief
    drew nigh to smite,
Spurring his horse, with resistless force against the
    Thane he thrust
With lance in rest and pierced his breast and pinned
    him to the dust.
And, as he shook the lifeless corse from the point of
    his blood-stained spear,
The Norman knights pressed forward and raised a
    joyful cheer,
And shouted, "Taillefer! Taillefer!": but the
    English stood astound
To see a second champion lie stretched upon the
    ground.

But from their midst, as they stood aghast, Leofwine
    strode in ire
And glanced at the corpses on the ground, while his
    blue eyes flashed with fire;
Then he fiercely turned to the triumphing knight, as
    he nigher came and nigher,
And poised a javelin o'er his head, steel barbed with
    a shaft of elm,
And launched it at the joint betwixt his hauberk and
    his helm.

It sped, as he shouted : "Juggling knight, go croak
    to the fiends of hell ! "
And swiftly smote right through his throat and,
    reeling from his selle,
Earthward rolled the minstrel bold and his armour
    clanged as he fell.
So Leofwine turned and left him there, the slayer
    with the slain,
And back to his post in the English host strode,
    singing a careless strain,
And his comrades cheered the valiant Earl, as he
    entered their ranks again.

But the Normans raised an angry shout, when they
    saw bold Taillefer fall,
And on they drave with spear and glaive against the
    bright shield-wall.
Swiftly they charged up the slope of the hill, while
    loudly the war-horns brayed :
They closed and the air was straightway filled with
    the clash of blade on blade,
As forward pressed the Norman knights and in air
    their falchions swayed
And smote at the shields and the wattled fence that
    guarded their English foes.
Over the din of the hurtling fight loudly their war-cry
    rose,

As fiercely they made at the stout stockade and shouted
    aloud : "Dex aie ! "

The earth grew red with a flood of gore and furious
    grew the fray,

As all along the English lines they hasted them on to
    slay.

But the terrible English axes flashed and grided on
    helm and shield,

And, wherever they smote, both horse and man went
    down on the blood-stained field :

Shields were shattered and helmets cleft, while ever the
    English shout

Cheerily rang o'er the clash of the steel : "Out ! "
    "Holy Rood ! " "Out, out ! "

And in the fight fell many a knight with helm or
    hauberk riven,

And the battle shouts and the clang of the fray went
    up to the face of Heaven.

Wave after wave of the Norman host surged up the
    slope of the mount ;

Fiercely they rode and fiercely smote, knight and baron
    and count :

But the English still on the brow of the hill blenched
    not a foot from their post,

Hurling them back from each fresh attack. As a cliff
    on the English coast,
When the south-west wind is singing aloft and the
    gray clouds cover the sky,
And the green seas, crested and flecked with foam, roll
    in as the tide runs high,
Waits till they dash on its weed-grown base, then
    shatters and flings them away
With a crash and a swash in a seethe of foam and a
    shower of wind-blown spray.

Ho! for the hissing javelin! ho! for the twanging
    bow!
Ho! for the arrows that darken the air and the shield-
    wall that fronts the foe!
Ho! for the sword that flashes and falls! ho! for the
    axe that bites!
Ho! for the blood that dyes the earth and the slaughter
    of Norman knights!
Fiercer and fiercer the battle grew; wilder the din of
    the fray.
"God Almighty!" "Notre Dame!" "Ha Rou!"
    "Out!" "Holy Rood!" "Dex Aie!"
Fitfully rose the mingled shouts, as English and
    Norman met
Hand to hand and axe to brand. The fight so fierce
    was set,

While neither side would yield a foot, that none who
    fought dared say
What flag would float, when the sun went down, o'er
    that red field of affray.

Right fiercely broke the wave of war on all the English
    front,
But in the centre of the field they bore the fiercest brunt.
There flew the banner that Rome had blest, and the
    prowest chivalry
The world could find couched lance behind the Duke
    of Normandy.
The greatest captain of his age was leading them on
    to the fray,
And lands and gold he had promised the bold, if he
    won a crown that day.
But vainly they strove to storm the height and the
    Duke waxed wild and wood,
As back they were thrust from the brow of the hill,
    where the flower of the English stood,
Shoulder to shoulder and shield to shield. For Harold
    the King was there,
And high on the hill his standards twain flaunted and
    flapped on the air.
The Golden Dragon of Wessex kings, that had ramped
    in many a fight,
And the king's own banner, his Fighting Man, that
    with gems and gold gleamed bright,

Rose up from the midst of a sea of steel ; and many a
    man must die
Ere they bowed to the banner that Rome had blessed,
    or the Norman chivalry.

But the eyes of the Duke were bright with wrath and
    a frown was on his face,
As he madly dashed at the baffling wall and smote
    with his mighty mace ;
His knights swept upwards after him, heads bent and
    lances low :
But the gleaming shield-wall met their charge and the
    javelins showered like snow
And the grinding axes rose and fell.   Before that grim
    array
The Normans blenched and left the Duke unaided in
    the fray,
As he battled like a paladin.   His steed was stricken sore
And, staggering back a yard or two, sank down in a
    pool of gore,
Horse and rider together locked.   The Norman knights
    drew rein,
When they saw him fall, and the cry went up : "The
    Duke ! the Duke is slain ! "
And thereat all along their line the tide of war rolled
    back
And the cause that had drawn them over sea had well-
    nigh gone to rack.

Meanwhile on the right, where the Bretons fought, it
seemed for a space as though

The bright shield-wall that crowned the hill had rolled
away the foe.

Thrice had they surged up the slippery slope, thrice
had they wavered back ;

Then awhile they halted at the base and shrank from
a fresh attack :

While, heedless of their King's command, the English
at the sight

Broke from the ground they should have held to make
that halt a flight.

They were pressing upon the wavering foe and forcing
them back amain,

When down the ranks there came the cry : "The
Duke ! the Duke is slain !"

In wild dismay the Bretons broke ; some stood, some
turned to run,

And the English pressed them eagerly and deemed the
day was won.

But the Bastard of Falaise was bold, as the flames of hell
are fierce ;

He rose unhurt from his slaughtered steed and uttered
a furious curse :

"Splendour of God ! I live, my lords ! Ye cowards,
will ye stay ?

I live ! and with the Saints to aid we shall retrieve the
    day ! ''

He gat himself another steed and brandished his sword
    in the air,

Then fiercely tore his helmet off and rode with his head
    all bare,

That all might know their Duke yet lived : so he
    checked each wavering knight,

Smiting them flatling as they fled and chiding left and
    right,

Until at length by voice and hand he stayed the tide
    of flight.

Yet still the English upon the right were driving the
    Bretons before

And still did the fate of a kingdom hang on the doubtful
    chance of war.

But, while he scarce could rally them, there came a
    shout of cheer,

As the valiant Bishop of Bayeux came galloping up
    from the rear,

Odo, the Duke's half-brother, with the rear-guard at
    his back

That the Duke reserved, lest evil hap should foil his
    first attack.

The warlike Bishop bestrode a steed that had better
    beseemed a knight

H

Whose trade is war, than a priest of God, unused to
    carnal fight :
A crozier of gold in his hand he bore, but a mace at
    his wrist was slung,
And under the snow-white aube he wore a warrior's
    harness rung.

To the right of the field his troops he wheeled, where
    the Bretons were flying apace
And the English with exultant shouts were holding them
    close in chase.
In an hour of ill had they left the hill, where the King
    had bidden them stay,
Losing the vantage of the ground and breaking their
    firm array.
In vain they strove to rally now, as the Bishop with
    sudden attack
Burst on the flanks of their scattered ranks and swept
    them struggling back.
The wall of shields was broken and the horse-hooves
    rang like thunder,
As the Norman knights came charging down and by
    sheer weight bore them under ;
Before them the ranks of the English bowed and earth-
    ward were they borne,
Like the ears of wheat when a flaw of wind sweeps
    over the standing corn.

The ears of wheat spring up again, when the flaw has
died away,

But the fallen English rose no more : for over them
as they lay

The Normans swept, a sea of steel, and beat them to
the ground.

Thus over a black and jagged reef the gray-green
billows bound ;

And the rocks that loomed awhile agone in a moment
are lost to sight,

While only a few dark points stand out, awash in the
seethe of white.

So here and there were a score or two, that with
shields together locked

Bore up for awhile, though the surging fight about
them reeled and rocked ;

And many a desperate deed was done, as they starkly
stood at bay,

Surrounded by the charging knights and the dust and
the clang of the fray ;

And, ere they fell outnumbered, was many a gory
lane

Gaped wide through the ranks of the Normans, strown
thick with a pavement of slain :

But few that had charged down the slope of the hill
won back to their comrades again.

So the flight of the Bretons was stayed at length and
    the battle rolled anew

Towards the summit of the hill, where the Dragon
    of Wessex flew.

" On ! To the standards ! " shouted the Duke : " On !
    To the standards, ho ! "

The cry was echoed along the line and fiercely they
    drave at the foe,

Flushed with the slaughter the Bishop had made, as he
    garnered a goodly tithe

From that harvest of death, where the Englishmen
    had fallen like grass to the scythe.

But the slope was still manned by a resolute band,
    and still rang the war-cry blithe :

"Out !" "Holy Rood !" and the shield-wall still rose
    grimly, a little aglint

In the light of the sun, as they breasted the hill and
    charged with a terrible dint.

Knight after knight came galloping up, whose fame
    flew far and wide,

And splintered his spear on the wall of shields, then,
    flinging the truncheon aside,

Smote with his falchion lustily.   But in vain their
    weapons clashed,

For the shield-wall stoutly held its ground and above
    it the axes flashed,

While death sat agrin on the grinded edge. The
 Norman lance and sword
Were harmless as reeds from a moorland pool : and
 many a Norman lord,
That had counted on winning fair leagues of land, as
 the meed of the toils he bore,
Gained nought but six feet of the English soil for his
 share of the spoils of war.

The Norman Duke chafed mightily, as charge after
 charge was foiled ;
A sullen fury burned in his eyes and the blood within
 him boiled ;
Forth to the front he spurred and stood, a target for
 the foe,
Waving his followers on to the hill where the banners
 blew to and fro.
But betwixt the Normans in the vale and the summit
 of the bent
Were the serried ranks of the English front, where
 the men of London and Kent,
The flower of the English army, fought in a grim,
 unbroken line
With the King's own brothers to captain them, Earls
 Gurth and Leofwine.
It was easy to point to the summit, but the slope was
 steep enow,

And the hedge that ran around it was hard to pierce, I
trow ;

Its thorns were sharp and set full close and the berries
that it bore

Were deadly as adders' poison and gay with the purple
of gore :

Goodly as glory were they to the show, but the taste
of them bitter as rue ;

For that hedge was a rampart of mail-clad men and
death was the fruit that it grew.

The two Earls marked the Norman Duke and they
knew their deadliest foe,

As forth he rode to the foot of the hill and pointed up
from below,

Reining his prancing charger in and halting full in
their view,

Heedless that thus he offered a mark for every shaft
that flew.

Each Earl upraised his javelin : first Leofwine's took
flight,

But by a hair's breadth missed the Duke and smote a
brave young knight,

Who, only a pace or two behind, was riding on his
right ;

And dead he fell from the saddle.   Then Gurth his
javelin cast ;

But, as he flung it, the Duke's horse reared at an arrow
    that whistled past :
So his aim was foiled and he failed of his mark, but
    full in his heaving chest
The snorting steed received the bolt that was meant
    for a nobler breast.

But the Duke sprang clear of his steed, as it fell, and
    cried to a Flemish knight :
"Now, lend me thy steed, Sir Rainulph, to bear me
    through the fight !
And, when I am crowned at Westminster, I will think
    of thy courtesy."
But the knight growled out : "No vassal am I of the
    Dukes of Normandy
And owe you never a heriot, Duke !" Dark grew the
    Norman's face,
As hoarsely he muttered : "Splendour of God !" and,
    lifting his mighty mace,
He starkly smote the mannerless knight and hurled
    him to the earth ;
Then into the empty saddle he leaped and rode up the
    hill at Gurth.

The Earl sprang out to meet him and aimed a mighty
    blow
That, had it struck the Norman full, had surely laid
    him low :

But he swerved aside and the axe fell short, yet smote
    him with such force

That the hauberk he wore was dinted in and back-
    ward he reeled on his horse.

But, bearing upon his stirrups and clinging to pommel
    and rein,

His seat he recovered and, ere the Earl could raise his
    axe again,

He dealt him such a terrible stroke that beneath it he
    staggered and fell

And was trampled under the horse's hooves.   There
    was none who saw could tell

Whether or no he died of that blow; but he fell and
    rose no more,

For onward over him where he lay rolled the tide of
    the Norman war,

As the Duke pressed gaily forward and shouted:
    "Dex Aie!   Dex Aie!

Lay on, lay on, my Normans bold!   Methinks ye are
    slack at the fray!"

While the English were daunted a little, when they
    saw how the Earl had sped,

And their ranks began to waver, as the tale of his
    death 'gan spread.

But Harold marked how they backward gave and
    heard the rumour that ran ;

So to the centre he hied him fast and, pressing through
     to the van,
Sprang fiercely at Duke William : but an eddy of the
     fray
Swept in between those captains twain and baulked
     him of his prey.
Then, raging like a wounded bear, he hurtled through
     the fight
And with his red, resistless axe felled many a daring
     knight,
While his voice rang like a thunder-peal : "Out!
     Holy Rood !   Out, out !"
The English saw his flashing axe and heard the ringing
     shout
And, rallying round the dauntless King, they beat off
     the attack.
The Norman Duke was swept away, as his knights
     went struggling back,
And the victory seemed distant still ; the royal diadem
Still mocked his greed : and, if his craft could find no
     stratagem
To shatter those stubborn ranks of steel, but little
     hope had he
To see again the pleasant plains of his sunny Nor-
     mandy :
For a hostile land encompassed him and the smiling,
     treacherous main.

But a cunning stroke of strategy was forming in his
    brain ;
And craftily he laid his plans, as he brought his
    troops to a halt,
And a little away from the foot of the hill took
    breath for a fresh assault.

Then up the slope with one accord they charged on
    every side
And with redoubled fury the fight raged far and wide.
The English met them stubbornly ; the battle-axes
    clave ;
The wall of shields still lined the ridge and shivered
    spear and glaive
And baffled the boldest riders : while, ever to the fore
Where the fight was hottest, Harold the king beat back
    the tide of war,
Stemming the onslaught of the Duke, as he threatened
    the English right.
At length along the centre the Normans turned to flight ;
Goodly the fare that was offered them there, but it
    seemed they had had their fill,
As horsemen and foot in a mingled crowd rushed
    headlong down the hill.

Small wonder if the English now were weary of
    standing at bay,

Tied to their post, while the foe ranged free! They
    had stood since break of day,
Galled by his ceaseless onslaughts, as he circled around
    the height:
But their blood was up when at last they saw the
    invaders full in flight.
So they paid no heed to Leofwine's voice, that
    shouted: "Stand your ground!"
For the cry went up, "They run! they run!" and
    the warning voice was drowned,
As they fell on the rear of the flying foe with spear
    and axe and brand,
Like a pent up river that bursts its banks and floods
    the level land.

The foe held on in sullen flight, drawing them over
    the field
Till they come where an ambushed squadron lay
    cunningly concealed:
Then the barons shouted: "Dex aie! Dex aie!" and
    suddenly round they wheeled
And halted, facing the scattered foe and drawing
    together their ranks;
While out from the ambush their comrades sprang
    and fell on the English flanks,
As they followed them flushed with victory. So, all
    too late they found

The trap they had fallen into. The vantage of the
   ground
Was theirs no more, while the foe closed in and
   pressed upon them sore.

Surprised, beset, outnumbered, yet fiercely they up-
   bore
On foot against the charging knights and dealt destruction dire.
They had no thought now of escape, but felt one
   fierce desire
To sate their wrath before they fell and send a long
   array
Of Norman knights to feed the kites that hovered
   over the fray.

So, leaving hope of life behind, they waded to their
   fate
Through a sea of Norman slaughter and glutted their
   fierce hate,
Mowing that field of death and doom, as the crisp
   scythes mow the hay.
The victor Normans fell in swathes, like the grass in
   June, and lay
In a grim and griesly carnage with a rich, red aftermath.

There were some, that knew the field right well,
   took flight but shaped their path

To a spot where the ground was broken by a gully
    dark and deep,
With trees and brushwood overgrown and its sides so
    sheer and steep
That a man might fall and perish there, ere he felt
    his footsteps sink ;
So the Normans, following heedlessly, plunged head-
    long over the brink.
Then the English wheeled upon them with a sudden
    and fell attack,
As they reined up their startled horses, and strove to
    turn them back ;
And many were slain by their onslaught, and many were
    forced by the foe
Over the edge to a hideous death in the charnel-house
    below.
They perished in such numbers there, that the gully
    was filled with the slain,
And, choked with the corpses of riders and steeds, lay
    level with the plain.

But their comrades, thirsting for revenge, thronged
    onwards undismayed
By the fury of the English, so the end not long was stayed;
For fivefold they outnumbered them and, fighting
    whiles they could,
The Englishmen were overborne and perished where
    they stood.

There were others had seized a hillock, that rose up
    out of the vale
And offered a little vantage ground, for its sides were
    steep to scale ;
And, flinging stones and javelins, they kept the foe at
    bay,
Till they gathered about them the scattered few that
    struggled out of the fray.
Then, locking their shields together, they formed up
    in a wedge ;
Its core was the fury of despair and it bristled with
    death at the edge :
And, shoulder to shoulder, they ran down the slope
    and battled towards the hill,
Where all that was left of the English host bore up
    unvanquished still.
But the Normans closed around them and the path
    was quickly barred,
And weary were they and wounded ; so the fight was
    going hard,
When Leofwine gathered a chosen band and to their
    rescue made,
Taking the Normans in front and rear : so with that
    timely aid
They hewed a path through the midst of the foe and
    out of the vale gat clear ;
A scant few saved from the rash pursuit that should
    cost all England dear !

So slowly through the valley the conflict died
away,
And against the hill the Norman Duke brought up his
whole array.

By this the English were too few to longer hold the
slope,
And the foe swarmed up on every side. Their hearts
beat high with hope,
As they mounted the steep that had baffled them long,
for at last the summit was won
They had striven to gain for seven long hours since the
rising of the sun.
But their warfare was not ended yet, for a grim, unbroken ring
Was gathered about the standards twain where battled
the English King.
His banners floated above him, as he marshalled his
array,
And the shield-wall still confronted them with a promise of stern affray,
Though many a shield was cloven, or riddled through
and through
With the spears that had shivered upon it and the
arrows of death that flew.
The victory still seemed distant, for fiercely as before
The conflict raged and the shield-wall still rolled back
the tide of war

Till again the Normans wavered and the tide of fight
    grew slack,
As charge after charge of their bravest knights was
    baffled and beaten back.

But the Duke has bidden his squadrons halt, while the
    archers ply the bow.
The arrows flew in a ceaseless flight like the flakes of
    the driven snow :
But they melted away like the driving snow, as the
    shield-wall met their flight,
And the English muttered : " It's little we reck, if they
    shoot till the fall of night."
But the Duke rode up to the archers and bade them
    shoot i' the air,
That their shafts might rain upon the foe and smite
    them unaware :
There was a pause for a moment, then, hissing down
    like hail,
The arrows showered from the sky above and smote
    through helm and mail.
A shudder ran through the English ranks and under
    that deadly rain
Their line began to waver and break, for the shields
    they bore were vain
To guard them 'gainst the double death, when, e'en as
    they struck at the foe,

Down from above fell those terrible bolts and smote
and laid them low.

Yet they rallied again to the voice of the King and
stoutly kept their ground

And, closing the gaps, still kept at bay the foemen
circling round.

But Fate had feathered an arrow with the downfall of
a realm.

As Harold battled with shattered shield and the crest
shorn off from his helm,

There was a cry; "Look up, my King! Look up
and guard your head!"

Woe for the thane that shouted and woe for the word
that was said!

The King upraised his cloven shield and flung one
glance on high,

One hasty glance, but the bolt smote down and quivered in his eye.

He staggered and clutched at the arrow and snapped
the shaft in twain

And flung it away; then, reeling back, sank down in
mortal pain

Betwixt his banners that streamed on the wind. So
England gat her bane!

There were twenty knights of the Normans had
banded themselves by an oath

That the life of the perjured English king should pay
for his broken troth.

Close together with spears in rest they charged when
they saw him fall ;

There were nine of them perished in the fray, but
they broke a gap in the wall

And rushed on the monarch as prone he lay.   Then
Leofwine sprang to his side

With the thane that had uttered that fatal shout and
they strove to stem the tide ;

And under the deadly blows they dealt the three that
were foremost died.

But there came a random arrow and pierced to the
heart of the thane

And fiercely the rest upon Leofwine pressed and the
gallant Earl was slain.

Then dauntless yet, though all was lost 'mid his
country's overthrow,

King Harold struggled to his feet and, striking one last
blow,

His battle-axe he shivered on the cloven head of his
foe :

And there betwixt the standards twain the Normans
ringed him round

And, raining upon him blow on blow, they beat him
to the ground.

A little the battle lingered yet, for the English
    scorned to run
And, stubbornly fighting to the last, they perished one
    by one :
So the Golden Dragon and Fighting Man, that had
    flaunted so long in the air,
Were hurled to the earth, as the setting sun went
    down with a lurid glare.

THE NIGHT OF THE BATTLE

The Golden Dragon is torn down at last,
    Never to float o'er battle-field again :
And from the captured mount the Normans cast
    The mangled bodies of the English slain.
Instead they raise upon the summit bare,
    Empurpled by the blood of King and Thane,
The Conqueror's tent ; that he may revel there
    On the red height, that saw till close of day
The flag of England fluttering in the air
    Over the last and fiercest of the fray ;
Waged by those dauntless few that scorned to yield,
    But perished round their monarch, as he lay,
Pierced by a thousand wounds, upon the field
Under the shards of his emblazoned shield.

Wide over Senlac heath a crimson flood
   Reddens the earth, wherever raged the fight,
And makes the vale a very lake of blood,
   Ghastly and glimmering in the cold moon-light,
That shines upon the relics of the fray :
   On slaughtered chiefs with faces wan and white
Upturned to heaven from the blood-stained clay ;
   On splintered spears and brands and dinted mail,
Heaped high where'er the English turned to bay.
   In blood-red characters is traced the tale
Of carnage : red as blood the watch-fires gleam
   Upon the victor's feast ; while in the vale
The English welter in the ensanguined stream,
And o'er the field the kites and ravens scream.

All night wild bursts of noisy revelry
   Sound from the hill and echo far away,
Where English thanes and Norman barons lie,
   Deaf to the jarring notes, in grim array.
Their flickering torches, flaming on the air,
   But half reveal the scene, yet strike dismay
To those two monks of Waltham and despair
   To Edith of the Swan-neck, as in vain
They search where hope is dead. No sign is there
   Of any living man o'er all the plain.
They will not find the King, will find at most
   A mangled corpse amid a pile of slain,

Where, like a King, he perished at his post
Betwixt the standards of the English host.

At length they wander towards the lofty mound,
    Where feasts the Duke in all a victor's pride.
The dead beneath its shadow pile the ground,
    Tossed by the conquerors ruthlessly aside
Into the reeking hollows of the dell.
    There sleep those English who unyielding died
In that grim carnage after Harold fell;
    And here at last the lurid torches shine
Upon those faces that they knew too well,
    The gallant Gurth and luckless Leofwine,
And, pierced and hacked by many a spear and brand,
    The best and bravest of Earl Godwin's line,
Harold the King, still clenching in his hand
His shivered axe, the sceptre of the land.

E'en then the ungenerous Conqueror's ruthless doom
    To the dead English king denied a grave
In consecrated earth.   A grander tomb
    The Heavens had destined for the free and brave.
Far from the haunts of men upon the lone
    Sea-coast he slumbers by the restless wave;
The island cliffs his monumental stone,
    The vaulted heaven his temple, while the sea,
Crooning a soft, sad lullaby, makes moan

As round his royal shrine she rolls.   So he
In death as life keeps watch and ward beside
   The island coast he kept so valiantly,
To guard whose ancient freedom he defied
The foe and dared the fight and, daring, died.

Printed by BALLANTYNE, HANSON & CO.
London & Edinburgh